01406985

Special Ed and Ginnie landed at their destination. They taxied over to the fuel farm to fill their tanks. That's where they met Sally the lady who was going to foster the puppies. They helped her load the puppies into her car and said goodbye. Another mission accomplished. Now it's time for lunch.

Special Ed and Ginnie took off without incident. They made it to their rendezvous destination with no further problems.

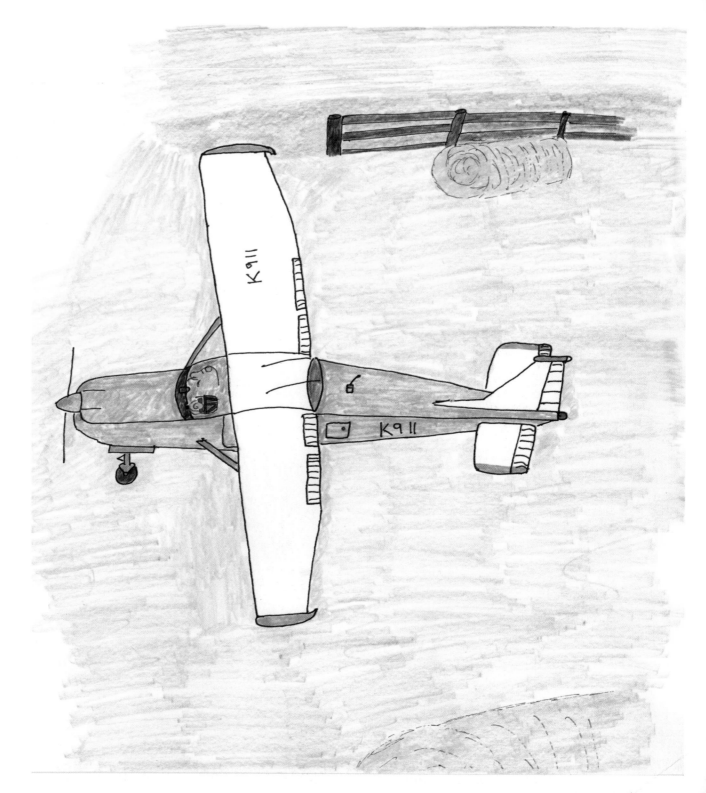

Imogene watched from the porch while they towed the plane to the pasture for takeoff.

Bluto rested in Imogenes lap. Imogene was impressed with his courage and adopted him Bluto felt safe and warm, in her lap. He felt no need to stand guard.

At breakfast Roy told Special Ed "that dog of yours is a dandy mechanic, but you need to brush her more often."

That made Special Ed Laugh.

Ginnie had the carburetor partially disassembled when Roy arrived.
She found the venturis clogged with fur, but the fuel filter was clean.
She figured she had left behind a fur ball the last time she changed
the air filter. Roy agreed with her.

Roy woke up early. Outside he saw a light on in the big barn. When he walked in he saw Ginnie repairing the plane by lantern light. He walked over to help her make the repairs.

Special Ed and Roy rigged the tractor to the plane using Special Ed's tow bar.
Roy then towed the plane into the big barn.

except Oscar who just wanted to play

and Bluto the runt who loved to stand guard

Most of the puppies were very tired and just wanted to sleep.

Imogene was in the kitchen. She welcomed Special Ed and Ginnie to her home. Then she showed Ginnie and the puppies to the kennel where they would stay with Gracie.

Ginnie explained to Gracie what she and Special Ed were doing. Gracie could not understand that there were people who did not love and respect their animals.

"You'ns O.K. over there" called Roy..

"We had some engine trouble but we're O.K." said Special Ed.

It's a gonna be a pourin he rain tonight, we etter put that airplane n the big barn" said Roy.

Farmer Roy was in the pasture mending fences and saw the whole thing.

Gracie heard a strange noise.

Clyde the draft horse watched the biggest bird he had ever seen land in the newly mowed pasture.

K911 glided right over Maydelle ,a particularl
disinterested cow.

Ginnie lowered the flaps.

On final approach Special Ed Kicked
a little right rudder to avoid the big
bales of hay.

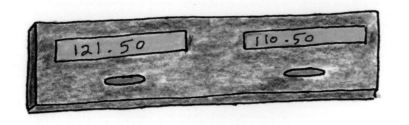

Special Ed turned the frequency dial of his primary transmitter to the emergency frequency 121.5, and called a Mayday.

Mayday, Mayday this is kilo niner one one making an emergency landing 10 miles northeast of London, Kentucky.

Special Ed then set the transponder to the emergency distress frequency of 7700.

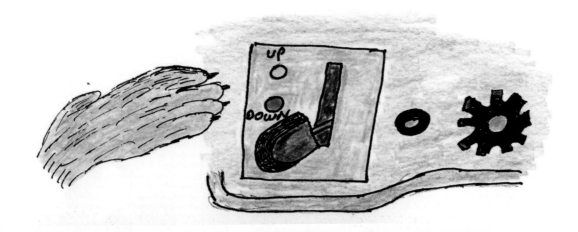

Ginnie lowered the landing gear.

"Well Ginnie, you know what to do" said Special Ed. Ginnie closed the Fuel mixture to full lean.

She turned the fuel selector valve from both to off

SpecialEd turned the ignition switch from start to off.

Ginnie slowly advanced the throttle from idle hoping for an engine restart.

The propeller turned freely but the engine never caught.

She pushed the fuel mixture in to full rich.

Special Ed pushed the primer to closed and locked it.

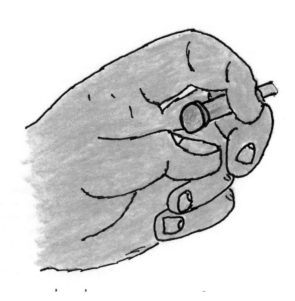

Special ed turned the ignition from both magnetos to Start.

But only for a moment. Special Ed immediately set the plane
up for the optimal glide speed of 75 knots. He looked around for a place
 to land. In the distance he spotted a pasture flat enough where
he could land into the wind. He knew they were too far from
the nearest airport to turn around and land there. He turned
towards the pasture.

Meanwhile Ginnie helped to get ready to try
to restart the engine. She checked to make sure
the fuel selector valve was set for both fuel
tanks.

The engine began to
sputter and quit.
Special Ed and Ginnie
looked at the inert
propeller in disbelief.

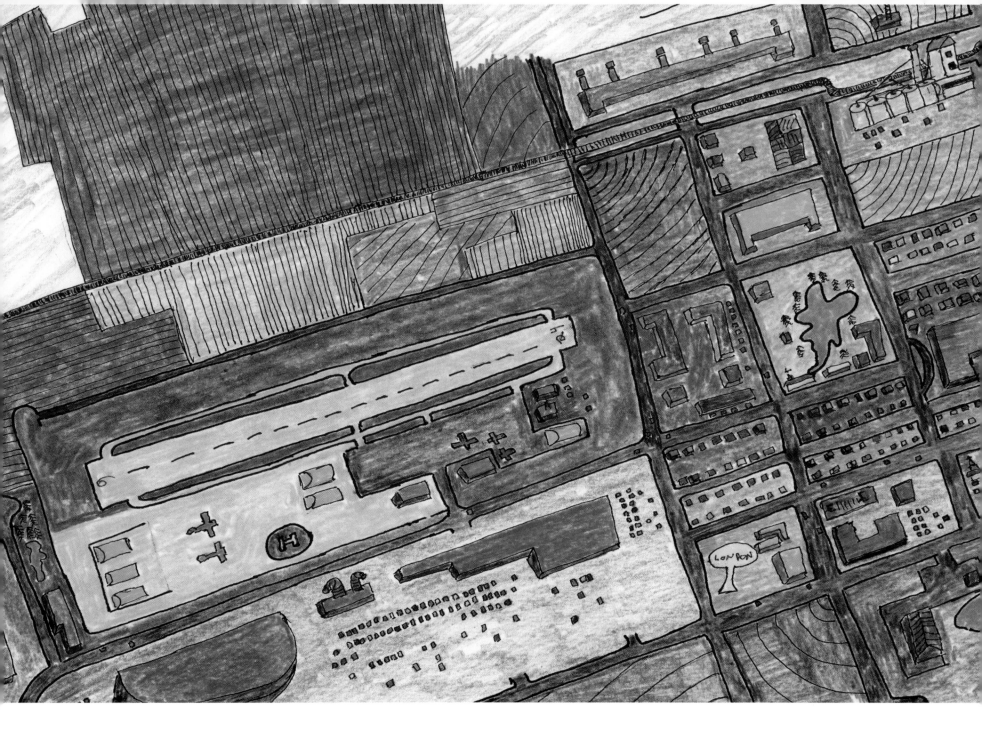

Special Ed and Ginnie had just flown over the airport nearest to them five minutes ago.

It was a beautiful day over eastern Kentucky

On board ,inside a big crate, on a big soft pillow were six very scared American pit bull terrier puppies.
They had never been away from their mommy before. One of Ginnies jobs was to help them feel more comfortable
 by being a substitute mommy for the trip. Their own mommy was at a veterinary hospital getting better.
Special Ed and Ginnie were moving them from an abusive kennel, where fighting dogs were raised ,to a foster home.
 They would never have to fight to entertain people.

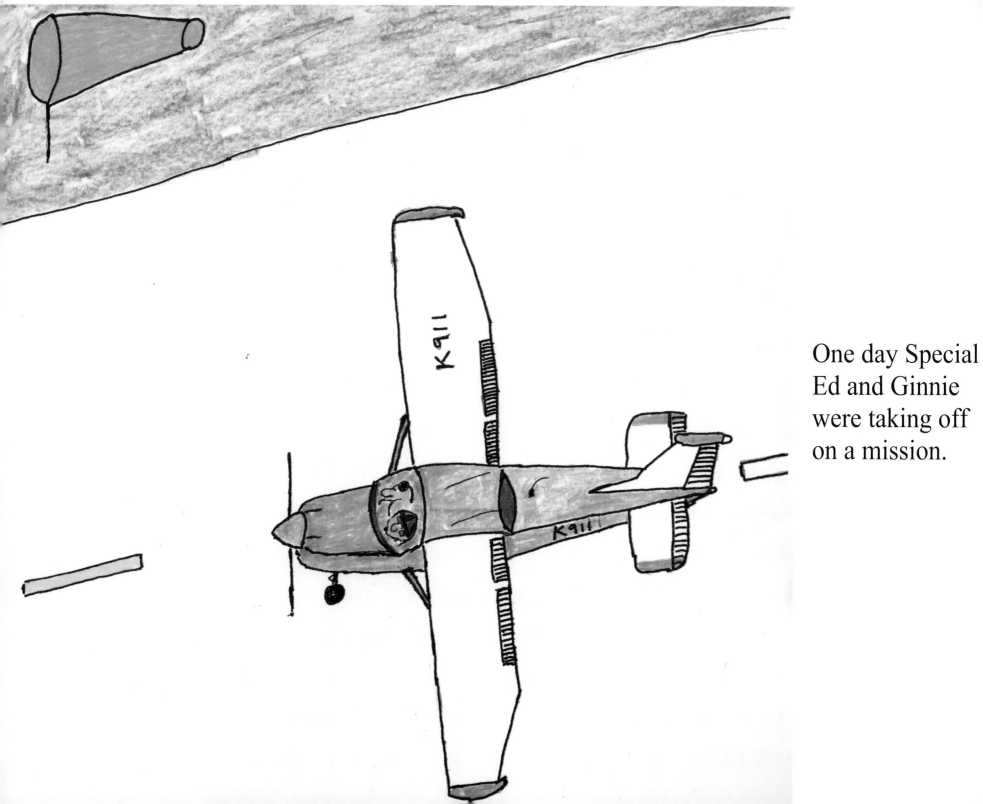

One day Special Ed and Ginnie were taking off on a mission.

Special Ed wasn't very bright, so he like having Ginnie as a copilot to help him fly. She was a good copilot and a good dog ambassador.

Special Ed loved Ginnie They had been flying together for a long time.

But mainly she liked to sit in the copilots seat ,and dream about the things she used to see from the air.

Ginnie didn't mind being blind.
She could still help Special Ed fly.

She could set the trim wheel.

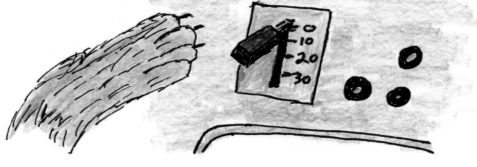

She could raise and lower the flaps.

She could raise and lower the landing gear.

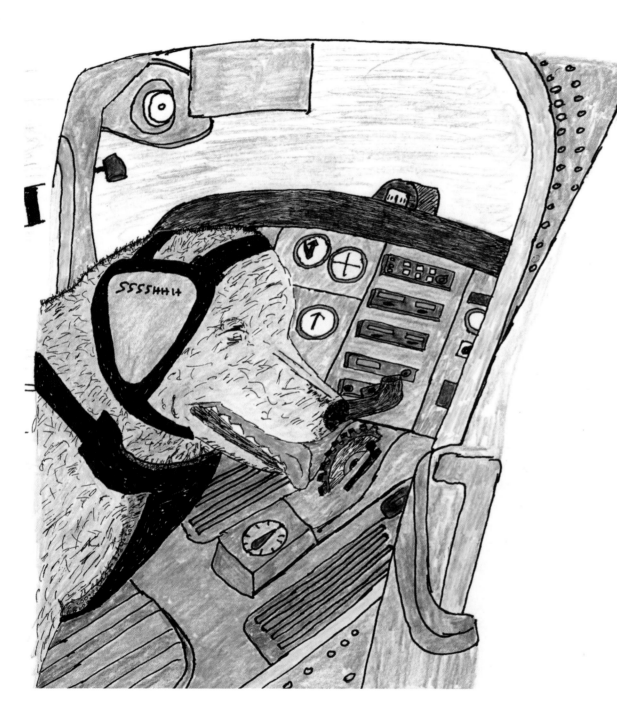

Ginnie was blind. She hadn't always been blind. She lost her vision late in life from a disease called glaucoma.

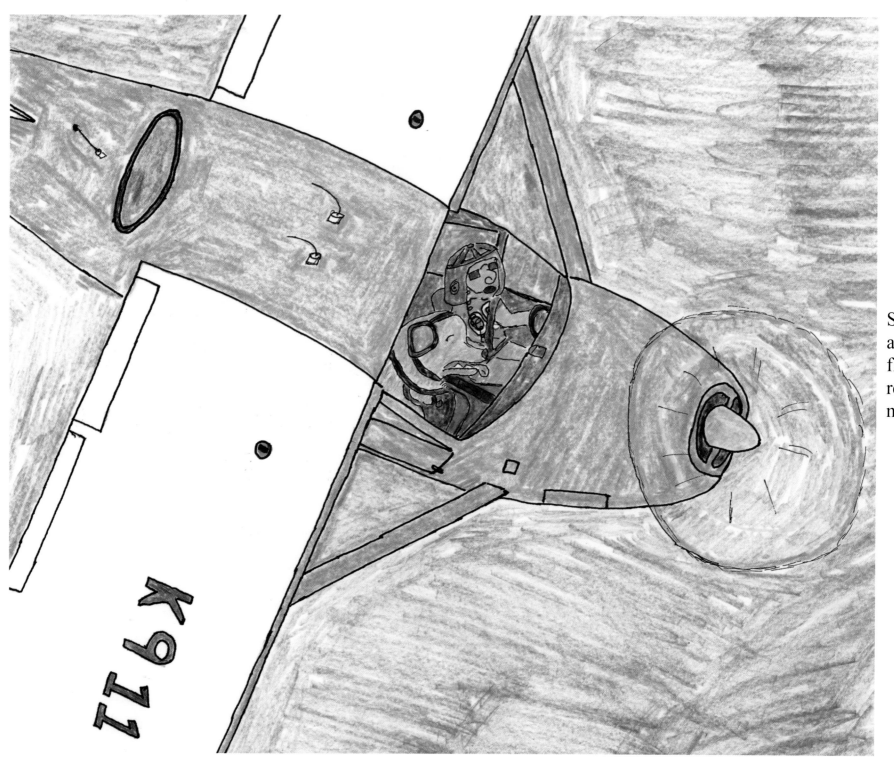

Special Ed
and Ginni
flew dog
rescue
missions.

All book sales benefit the K-9 Underground Railroad

Printing in the United States by BookMasters, Inc.
30 Amberwood Parkway
Ashland, Ohio   44805
August 2011
Job Number: M8799

ISBN: 978-1-4507-8597-6